First First Love

The dawn of togetherness

Walter Eastwood

Publisher: Walter Eastwood

Walter Eastwood 2025

Print ISBN: 979-89910165-3-7

eBook ISBN: 979-8-9910165-4-4

Copyright TXu 2-476-136

All rights reserved. No part of this publication may be reproduced, distributed, or transmitted in any form or by any means, including photocopying, recording, or other electronic or mechanical methods, without the prior written permission of the publisher, except in the case of brief quotations embodied in critical reviews and certain other noncommercial uses permitted by copyright law.

Contents

Chapter-1-Questions......................4

Chapter-2-Who Are They…………...12

Chapter-3-Clans………………….....14

Chapter-4-Its Not Evil, Its Survival…24

Chapter-5-Impetus………………....33

Chapter-6-Is There A Difference……39

Chapter-7-Food Or Fire...…………...46

Chapter-8-The Miricle Of Willow…..56

Chapter-9-The Mending…………….62

Chapter-10-Are You Seeing this….…67

Chapter-11-Can You Count………….73

Chapter-12-End or Beginning……….83

Chapter 1

Questions

Eighty thousand years before this story begins, and not long after the ice began to recede, two distinct groups of humanoids walked together, sharing very different worlds. The Cro-Magnons arrived later and maintained their distance due to a natural fear of the unknown. They had seen firsthand the Neanderthals potential for treachery. Using clubs and spears, they brought down a giant beast on which they fed. The new man, ever wary, stayed out of sight to learn their ways.

It didn't take long for the new race to refine their methods, and their immense success led to a significant decline in the numbers of the Neanderthals. The older race was more cautious and soon found themselves forced further north, living on the edge of extinction under the shadow of the great ice walls.

Not one member of early humans could recall why they kept their distance from each other. During their treks to and from the hunting fields, they would often cross paths. The Magnon leader, who is also Kara's father, on his best day was an imposing figure, and often scolded her about being friends with the Neanderthals.

As they journey through the intermittently sheltered forest, they once again cross paths with their neighboring clan of Neanderthals. On this day, they working their way through a barren stretch of rocks, untouched by the cold runoff. The small blonde girl noticed the stark difference between them and people of Kara's clan: they were shorter, bulkier, and mostly covered with hair.

She had seen them before, but never this close. She couldn't decide which of the two clans was braver. Kara looked to see if Drud was watching her, so she raised her hand ever so slightly and waved at the only person who had ever looked her way. She was delighted when the boy waved back. Warmed by her uncommon friend's acknowledgment, she gasped at the silhouette of his clan breaking the whiteness of the glacier miles behind them as they continued on their trek to wherever they camped.

Kara had a puzzled expression on her face; she looked back and forth at the very different groups of hunters. Both were transporting the remains of their kill, as they balanced the meat on their shoulders. She also noted that the size difference of the Neanderthals' required fewer men to carry what looked like an equal amount of flesh. Despite her youth, an idea began to form in her mind. A quick calculation convinced her that there must be a better way to transport the game. Predators, whether walking or stalking, constantly posed a danger to their camp. If there was a way to free up even one man, it could provide some security.

Her clan had finished the day's hunt, which yielded an exceptionally large woolly rhinoceros. They had to stay vigilant due to the abundance of large carnivores lurking among the deep grasses within the sheltered forest. Enormous sabretooth cats, capable of annihilating them all, sometimes flocked to the free meal they were transporting.

Even though the felines are capable of attacking and killing the rhinos, killing a few humans was so much easier. Besides, there was no need to gnaw through the heavy hide; it was just lying there, all neatly butchered. This time of year, the large female cat usually has cubs that are easily capable of chewing through the flesh of insignificant humans. Maybe she would let them eat them later, as dessert. What a treat! She, of course, will have the first bite.

Thinking of this, Kara shifted her attention to watching their surroundings. This time her father gave her permission to join in the hunt and named her as one of the four lookouts. Think of it like the canary in the coal mine; there were three other children that walked a dozen or so yards at the perimeter edge as a sacrifice to the gods they do not yet believe in. Losing a child was an acceptable loss to ensure that the clan made their way back to camp with fresh meat intact. Besides, they haven't lost a child in more than two warm seasons.

Kara cringed; fear overwhelmed her; she had heard a disturbance somewhere behind her. She looked back to where she had last seen the alien clan. She was shocked to see Drud rushing toward her. His wide-eyed expression confused her. Suddenly, concentrated on Drud, she did not hear her father's loud footsteps until he rushed by her. She watched as he raised his arms, expecting an impact that would kill her distant friend. She was surprised and frightened even more when she looked up to see Drud running toward her with a spear raised high. Was he angry with her?

Her heart was pounding; she looked toward the sound of her clanmates rushing toward her, their faces etched with urgency. They too passed by her and went to where her father and Drud stood, they were separated by the body of a large cat. Standing over the beast was the boy; he had seen that she was in peril and closed the distance between her and the prowling cat. He had managed to strike him dead with a spear the size of their leader's club. Her father was standing on one side of the bleeding beast, while Drud was on the other. The cat had his spear embedded in its body, while her father's smaller spear lay on the ground a meter away.

The boy stood rigid, guarding his kill; Erg, their clan leader, was cautiously approaching from behind the amazing hunter. Her father nodded his admiration, and if he could speak, he would have thanked him for saving his daughter's life. Although the two different species have shared the land for thousands of years, her clan were still the interlopers.

On these occasions, they would share in the bounty. Kara never knew when the need to share began, maybe it was due to similar events that had just passed, but she was glad that her friend was not going to be killed this day. Actually, she had only heard tales of a time when the two species would have open battles. She suspected that it was not her clan who started the odd peace between them. Despite their smaller stature, any one of them was as strong as three of theirs.

While her clan regrouped after all the excitement was over, Kara looked back and watched the boy and others dragging the big-toothed cat back to their camp. Her clan rarely ate the flesh of carnivores; obviously, her friend did not have the same objections. She waved; he was not looking back. She followed in behind the retreating troop, and took the position a few dozen yards behind them.

There was still a job she had to do after all.

Chapter 2

Who Are They

Kara, a bright, precocious teen on the cusp of becoming the first thinker who may elevate her clan of Cro-Magnon men out of the constant danger they live in. Kara is as tall as her father, Ando, and much taller than her soon-to-be friend, Drud. She is thin and sinewy, whereas he is short and bulked up with bulging short muscles.

Drud, Kara's friend, is a Neanderthal from a different clan and species. They have never met; they wave to each other in passing. His hair covers his body, enabling him to withstand the harsh winters. Kara and her people are pretty much hairless and must resort to applying furs to their bodies to fend off the cold.

Ando, Kara's father, is the leader of their clan. He is without a mate, as a hunt claimed her mother's life years ago. The death of her mother was the impetus behind her mental growth.

Drud's clan lives near the base of a receding glacier, a spot chosen for the modicum of protection it offers at their rear. They need only to watch the south, where the sun rises and sets, to get a panoramic view of any approaching dangers. The rocky open expanse between the base of the glacier, where plants and trees have yet to encroach, adds to their defense. They have abandoned their caves long ago due to the territorial invasion of the tall clansmen, who applied pressure on their ecological existence.

Chapter 3

Clans

The two competing clans are unalike in so many ways, yet they are similar in an equal number of ways. The Magnons are relatively new to the world, and have made so many advancements in hunting. By adding seeds into their diet, they have generated a practical sustainability lacking in the Neanderthals, which is another reason for the threat of the Neanderthals vanishing into the past.

Both clans understand that autumn will soon be on them. The heat coming from the sun will soon wane along with the receding light. Except for the early days of thawing and the sprouting of new life, the skies are clear of clouds. Kara can't get enough of the intermittent warm days. Hunting and gathering seeds take up most of her time. When the hunters are away, only the older clansmen and women stay in the camp to fulfill ancillary needs for the clan.

The men and women of their clan need to wear longer-fitting outerwear, while the Neanderthals have very little need to clothe themselves. While the troupe hunts or reaps, the elders are preparing meals, fabricating clothing, making repairs to their huts, or building better weapons. The clan is large enough to have a need for two Knapper's.

The Magnons spear points are long and thin and very refined; on the other hand, the Neanderthal's weapons are large shards of stone crudely affixed to a tree limb or some other type of lever. Nevertheless, both styles of weaponry are adequate enough to effectively supply their clans with an acceptable supply of meat.

Given their relative frailty compared to the Neanderthal's, the Magnons are compelled to hurl their weapons at whatever beast passes their way, of which they have become specialized in doing so. On the other hand, the Neanderthal bashes their prey to death, which often results in a casualty; even death can occur. If there were some real deep thinkers in their group, they would learn from the Magnon's and take down game from a distance. The clan's numbers are slowly diminishing due to their continued use of present methods and the risks they take.

The training of clan members varies between the different species and the competing clans. The Neanderthals use the hunt-from-afar method in conjunction with the passing down of lore through the oral gestures and sign talk. Spoken words are beyond their abilities, although there are vocal nudges that are as effective as the spoken word. Give them a few thousand more years, a more expansive language may have developed. Despite their grunts and shoving, they passed on life lessons, which kept them alive until the competition from the new comers started to infringe upon their existence.

Life in both clans mirrors each other closely in their daily routines and survival strategies; it's their techniques that create a contrast. They can be likened to the big cat family. A tiger and a lion are distinct species within the Panthera genus. While they share similar hunting skills, one of them has evolved to go beyond the primitive method of jumping on its prey and bludgeoning it to death. Neanderthals and Cro-Magnon, too, exhibit striking resemblances but have diverged significantly in their methods and adaptations, much like how our distinct families thrive in the savannas and rugged mountains of their habitats.

There is still an abundance of game animals to hunt. A few thousand years ago the Cro-Magnons arrived from warmer climes somewhere east of the Mediterranean Sea. At first there was curiosity and even an exchange of gifts, a goodwill gesture. Nobody knows how the eventual separation took place, but there may have been a death involved. Perhaps it involved a hunting accident or a squabble over a joint kill. Regardless, two millennia later, there is still an unspoken rift between the two clans.

The period between then and now was a time when the new people, unfamiliar with the terrain and associated danger, studied the ways of the Neanderthals and learned much from them. There were spontaneous, unspoken ideas that popped into a clansman's head, and changes were made to equipment, methods, and means propelled the new people into a better position. That too may have worsened the rift. It has been in the last few hundred years that things between the clans began to cool off. Ceding the big cat to Drud would have been unheard of even as late as fifty years ago.

The question of how fire became a useful tool that saved both clans is still inadequately answered. It could have been a random find, such as a red deer that died in a forest fire. One of the ever-hungry clansmen, tasted the cooked meat and was pleased. Preferring the taste of cooked meat over raw, he may have then collected burning embers and somehow brought them back to camp, and from there it became a way of life.

Fire was important to both clans in ways other than cooking. In addition to keeping them warm during cold nights, fire also served as a deterrent to predators, with the ancillary benefit of keeping animals at bay while they slept. It was a powerful tool used for herding prey toward cliff edges where they plunged to their deaths on the rocks below. Clans sharing was practical during times of bounty. Both understood that wasting meat was unacceptable, and at those times, forced friendship was acceptable. Perhaps this was the beginning of their acceptance of each other's company.

Survival depended on the hunts, especially for the Magnon's, not so much for the Neanderthals. They were forced to hunt in order to supplement their herbivorous diet with meat for their survival. Even though time has passed, and the weather was ideal for gathering food stores, the killing of beasts continued.

There was a list of activities that would fill their days. While the hunters were away, those left in the camp worked diligently while waiting for their return. They divided their tasks; first, they would skin hides from earlier hunts and then stretch them out in the sun to dry. After stretching, a thick layer of sand they had collected from the river banks was spread over the hide. There was a sufficient amount of salt in the sand to properly tan the hides.

Then there were the berry pickers, nut collectors, and the wheat-berry gleaners. Early craftsmen who kept the camp in good repair, like a condo maintenance man. Naturally, they were also responsible for crafting weapons. Without them, the clan would dwindle in size due to their inability to collect sufficient amount of protein.

Men stationed around the Magnon group were there to protect the camp from predators and hungry clansmen from other regions. Those encounters were often brutal, as they always involved individuals belonging to their own species. As menacing as the Neanderthals appeared to be, they did keep to themselves. For lack of a better science, it was as if they knew better.

At times, Ando would require his men and young females to cross the open plains south in the direction of the big mountains, even though most wanted to stay near the comfort and safety of their camp. At least three warm cycles separated these treks, never exceeding five. These required treks involved necessary contact with other clans who were sometimes unfriendly. The real purpose of these gatherings was to trade off women of the clan to ensure diversity. There was an exception: the senior female in the camp was brought along to approve all trades.

Kara's mother came from one of those gatherings. It wasn't something her father instigated; it was an event that was passed down from their earlier leader. They didn't elect Ando, nor was leadership passed down through family. He was leader only because he was the strongest clan member. And as time went on, fighting for leadership was too costly to lose even one clan member. Hence, it was inevitable; succession was a given fact.

On occasion, there would be periods of sickness. Usually those events occurred after their return from a gathering of clans. Sporadically, the clan would suffer a loss of members. One time a catastrophic die-off occurred, decimating the clan, it had taken several generations to grow their numbers, ensuring the viability of the clan. It was after that episode that things changed.

Natural selection has shaped the clan's limited social structure. Members of size were automatically designated hunters; smaller members tended to the clan's well-being. Over the centuries, people became more adept at their forced life choices. Those who were proficient in food preparations took charge of food storage. Those who could heal became wildcraft foragers and medicine men or women. They viewed no group as superior to another; they were a single organism. This was not the case for the designated leader. The clan set him apart, kept him at metaphorical distance and showed no favoritism to anyone, including Ando's daughter.

Further north, the Neanderthals functioned on a different level. That evolutionary tract was on a simpler and more pragmatic path.

Chapter 4

It's not evil, Its survival

In our two samples of humanoid life, religion has not yet manifested itself; the later events are uncommon but crucial. While each clan has the ability to repel predators, we must approach the introduction of any food source that poses a risk to either clan with pragmatism. On this day in the camp of Magnons, a small child is gravely ill. A slow, quiet death for one so young is tragic enough; however, they cannot allow a weak, screaming child to attract unwanted predators.

Shortly after the last clan gathering, Wend's daughter fell ill with an apparent painful affliction, which she expressed through uncontrollable sobbing. Wend's mother had taken the girl to the far reaches of the camp in an effort to isolate her because she knew that her cries would be a problem if they were to continue. So she found a spot near the high rocks where she could see all around her front side without having to look over her shoulder.

Despite holding an axe in one hand and her baby in the other, the mother had no chance of saving her own life, let alone that of her child, should one of the large cats pursue them. She bravely sat, eyes wide, listening for hidden dangers in the moon-filled night until the snap of a branch sent fearful chills up and down her spine. She did something so natural; she heaved her weapon at the sound coming from the direction of her sleeping clan.

In a moment of anticipation, she forced her back into the solid rock as if it would protect her and her child. She turned away, shielding her child who had yet to stop wailing. Maybe the beast would be satisfied with her and leave the child unharmed. Then a warm hand grasped her shoulder. It was the hand of a man; feeling safe, she opened her eyes and looked into the face of Ando, her leader. He slowly pried the crying infant from her grasp. If he had a word to express what he felt, it might have been, "I'm sorry."

His next step had nothing to do with an invisible God, nor was there an imperative to save the dying child. What Ando was about to do had everything to do with protecting his clan.

Holding the child in his arms, he placed his hand on Wend's shoulder once more. She then sat back and began to cry softly. She watched her leader walk out into the night, away from camp. What he is doing has happened so rarely that most clansmen could not relate. It was an innate sense of survival, not something passed down from one generation to another.

Once he returned to the well-worn trails from years of hunting, the darkness did not deter him. Ando did not know fear; he needed to take the threat that faced his clan to an area that would isolate his people from danger. On occasion, when he needed quiet, he went to a place that he had found long ago, a stretch of flat land atop a high hill that was littered with the bones of every animal found in their kingdom. The beasts must have come to this place to meet their natural end. He's uncertain, yet somewhat confident that any beast who ascended this climb had no desire for a last meal.

He carried the child into the center mass of bleached bones. He laid the still wailing child on a bare, damp area of grass. He then began to build a nest of sticks and dry grasses. The baby continued wailing. Just as he was about to finish, the child abruptly stopped crying. It would have been a relief if it were not for the sound of someone or something approaching.

Unlike Wend, Ando turned to face his attacker; he froze, not out of fear but at the sight of the Neanderthal leader approaching. His worry vanished as fast as it appeared; what he realized was that the clan leader was also carrying a sick child in his arms. It became clear that he, too, had the responsibility to protect his people.

It wasn't like they were having a standoff. The instant understanding compelled the two antagonists to give it a rest. Ando nodded, and Erg acknowledged his welcome and stepped forward. His child looked to be in the same condition as his own. Ando stepped aside and allowed the leader to rest his child beside his in the improvised cradle. They each turned to one another, nodded and grunted in their non-verbal way of communicating, then walked away into the darkness. A sadness filled their hearts.

If not for the curiosity of two adolescents, that would have been the end of it. In the quiet of the night, Kara had been awakened by the ever-crying child, so she had taken herself to the edge of safety and sat under a giant tree. Often vivid pictures formed in Kara's mind, and this night was no exception. Although she had covered enough ground to dampen the sounds of the crying baby, suddenly the wailing seemed to be coming closer. She began to stand and then collapsed back against the tree, trying to blend into the background. In the moonlight, she saw her father making his way towards the high ground, carrying the sick child in his arms. There was sadness on his face. She was puzzled, he had always had one look, and that was determination.

Unbeknownst to them, across the hunting fields, another sick child from the other clan was being removed. By a strange coincidence, Drud was imitating Kara as he trailed his leader out of their camp into the darkness. He, too, stayed in the shadows and waited. Bewildered at the sight of the tall Magnon, he mistakenly thought that there was some kind of ritual about to be performed. As curiosity overtook him, he was about to follow but then suddenly froze in his steps. His leader was taking the same path and carrying a child as well.

Once the two leaders had left the children behind, it was as if they were at the starting line of a one-hundred-yard race. Both observers sat in silence until the danger of being caught was nearly impossible. Then, they sprinted to the abandoned children at precisely the same time. The sound of their feet smashing onto the ground worried them both, but the intensity of their emotions prevented them from hearing each other's footfalls.

As the two caregivers approached, the children, seemingly aware that salvation was imminent, ceased their crying and lay silently. At that moment, the far-off friends stood together on the ossuary of death; they were but a few feet apart. They stared into each other's eyes for a long moment, then Kara lowered herself and on bent knee, she gently lifted her clanmate off the makeshift crib. Drud followed suit and now they were standing side by side, looking back to their respective camps.

Kara was the first to move; she turned and walked off into the night, holding the little waif in her arms in a direction 90 degrees from both camps. Neither child had moved or cried since they first stood over them. At this point in time, the two clans, out of necessity, developed a rudimentary form of communication over the years. What little they had did not actually translate effectively. Therefore, Drud maintained a short distance behind his friend and followed her to wherever she was about to lead him.

After the great sacrifice, Ando was the first to notice his daughter's absence the following morning. Unlike in modern times, there was no shrieking and shouting, "My baby, my baby!" There was the ever-stoic Ando expressing an ever-present anger at his child, who has shown many signs of transitioning into womanhood. It was probably one of those times when it's best to leave her be and let her work out whatever issues she is confronting.

On the other side of their small world, Erg went about his daily task of counting heads; occasionally, a large cat would sneak into camp and steal a sleeping child. He noted with sadness that he was one clansman short, and he had been one of his favorites. As it is in the Magnon's camp, he shook it off as another worrisome loss to the wilds.

Kara and Drud awoke in the coolness of a small cave they had taken refuge in during the morning hours, grappling with the dilemma facing them. They had laid the children between them, keeping them warm. They were both smiling; well, Kara was, she didn't think Neanderthals could smile; although, she could detect relief in his eyes. The uncertainty of their next course of action troubled her. Drud, on the other hand, pointed to a far forest and looked to Kara for approval.

Chapter 5

Impetus

It is said that necessity is the mother of all inventions, and at this point in time, with two sick children, the four castaways sure could use that mother now. On their second morning, Kara had woken before the rise of the sun. She was on her knees, at the side of her new family, watching them sleep. The moment she placed the children side by side, they miraculously stopped displaying symptoms. It was as if their touch was all the medicine needed.

She studied Drud's face in the dim light of their temporary home. The cave was small, too small to be a den for the giant bear, she thought.

However, she realized that a giant bear could provide them with sustenance for all eternity. This fleeting notion abruptly jolted her back to the present and their pressing need for food.

Kara was ankle-deep in a small stream when Drud found her. He did not need to ask her what she was doing; he had watched her clan do this before. Fish did not even constitute a minor portion of their diet, as Neanderthals were notoriously poor fishermen. She was constructing a low weir just beneath the water's surface, angling it diagonally across the stream to guide fish into a small hollow at its end.

A surprisingly short time later, Drud and Kara were wading downstream in knee-deep water. Using their hands to agitate the water, they moved toward the trap she had created. Though they didn't know if they'd catch a fish, it was fun and provided them with much-needed relief from their new untested life. To both adventurers, what they found in the shallow hollow was a delightful surprise. There were four large rainbow trout sloshing around in circles with no way out.

The young parents realized that their joining could not have been more fortunate; they had both innate and learned skills. Kara walked along the stream's edge, looking for the right rock. She had watched every clansman doing their specific task and tried to mimic it. One of her observations was watching knappers perform their craft. With glee, she snatched a big piece of flint from its resting place and held it high in the air. Her second significant step forward in as many days.

Drud tore at the fish, trying to rip the flesh free. Kara placed her hand on his shoulder; he stopped and looked up. When she showed him her stone, he relaxed and sat back on the sand. At that moment, she realized communication would be a problem. She raised the flint in the air and made a striking motion, trying to convey what she needed to do to prepare the fish. He shrugged, as if giving her the floor.

Away from the stony beach was an area filled with granite rocks. Although the granite rocks weren't ideal for knapping, she understood that perfection wasn't necessary for its intended purpose. She had seen how the knappers would place a flint between their knees, then use them as a vise; they would strike the flint along an edge, causing a shard to break free. Each shard was in itself a sharp cutting tool. She did not need a fully crafted knife; she needed only one cutting tool to prepare their first meal.

After fire entered their lives, Kara had become accustomed to eating cooked meat, while Drud had no trouble eating raw fish. It was time to start a fire, not only for cooking purposes but also to ensure the cave remained warm for the children. The worry of feeding them vanished as each child eagerly devoured their part of raw flesh. Now her thoughts returned to fire.

In the Neanderthal's camp, once fire was lifted from the floor of a burning forest, it was kept alive by a tender whose responsibility was to keep it burning. In her clan, they had learned to start a fire by striking flint against a shiny rock. She already had the flint; what she needed to do was find a piece of shiny rock. She gestured to Drud, asking him to take care of the children for a moment. She hurriedly returned to the rock pile, and she began looking for the shiny rocks. A fire needed to be burning this night; they were not yet ready for any cold spells. In their haste to save the children, they did not pack a suitcase, as it were.

Puzzled by the absence of shiny rocks she needed, she ventured into the tree line and beyond. She had no weapons, and danger lurks in the shadows, but she must find the rock. A few paces in, she neared a washout, where rainwater spills over a high cliff. The spillway formed a depression where the soil had been washed away, leaving a stony bed of rocks. There were so many shiny rocks, it looked like a bejeweled basin filled with enormous wealth. What she was looking at was a lifetime supply of iron pyrite. There would never be a need to search for this valuable asset ever again. It was time to start a fire.

Chapter 6

Is There A Difference?

Both clans have a unique structure that may require them to pause their daily lives and search for any missing members. Understand that each member has specific responsibilities that are important to their continued survival. In the Magnon's camp, there are always two knappers. Since they have a backup, they can tolerate the loss of one knapper, ensuring the craft stays intact. Due to their diminishing numbers, the Neanderthals' counterpart would be the skinner whose dual job is to make weapons and tools out of bones from earlier hunts. The absence of redundancy is an issue for them.

In both camps, whether by design or reasoning, and if possible, all jobs are redundant except for the healer. For obvious reasons, no one puts their lives in danger. Kara, an apprentice healer, has disappeared. Unlike Kara, Drud is merely a future hunter, and his loss won't have a significant impact on the lives of his small clan. But Kara's absence has a detrimental effect on their immediate future, especially in the coming weeks and the next hunt.

Lod, the aging healer in the camp, sought answers from Ando, but the big man rudely ignored her. She was angry enough to pop him upside the head with her walking stick that sometimes doubled as a billy club when events called for it. It was never a good idea to rile their leader; she assumed that he knew Kara's whereabouts and that at some point he would relate it to her, or Kara would simply show up. Lod was concerned about the loss of her apprentice; if she didn't return, she wouldn't have the time to train another at her age.

In the other camp, the missing Drud was not a concern; members were often killed or dragged off into the fearsome night. The positive aspect was that Burge would be joining the next hunt, a prospect he welcomed as he disliked the tedious nature of berry picking.

Everyone in both camps seemed to understand the disappearance of the infants, as has occurred many times in the past. All sorts of carnivores, especially the hyenas who never ventured too far from either camp, could easily take advantage of a noisy child. Because everyone must complete everyday tasks, watching the children took on a special significance.

As the next in line advanced, the daily struggles of the missing older children quickly faded from memory. Only Lod felt a loss. Kara was arguably the most intelligent Magnon in their short history, and her replacement would be decided by the age of the next in line, not by a rigorous test. She was smarter than anyone she had ever met, in or out of the clan.

Lod was the clan's healer; she too had fallen into her duties by being the next in line. That was extremely fortuitous for the clan because of her innate ability to understand the complexities of early medicine. She had learned a modest amount of her practice from her teacher, who was not a caring practitioner. During her apprenticeship, she would always, without fail, receive a slap across her face whenever she made a mistake. Nevertheless, she acquired knowledge and developed her craft independently by employing basic experiments. Her rapid growth relegated her mentor to cleaning up after hunts, and her sewing skills led her to become a basket maker.

She found many applications for hides and innards. She was a much happier person in her new field of expertise.

Following her mentor's removal, Lod became the clan's sole healer or medicine woman. She came to view Kara as a gift, despite her initial disinterest in her new responsibilities. She greatly enjoyed hunting in the steppes with her father; however, she quickly became involved in her work after helping Lod mend a small child's broken arm.

After that, her small rebellion came to an end, and she dove into all she could learn from her advanced teacher, and learn she did. It took her less time to master the totality of the clan's knowledge than it did Lod. It wasn't long before she was doing experiments on her own. She often worried about the safety of the hunters and her father in particular. She knew that at some point she would be tending to his injuries. There must be a more efficient and safer method of hunting the big animals the clan depended on for survival.

Her father was such an inspiration to her. She would watch him as he occasionally strayed away from the hunt to study the methods used by the Neanderthals. He quickly understood the need for hunting larger animals. Although dangerous, hunting larger animals provided greater amounts of meat, ensuring clan survival. Kara worried about her father's potential injuries, so she began to focus on improving hunting techniques.

Which brings us back to the problem before her now. When she was in one of her thought experiments where she would try to advance an idea by visualizing desired results using various methods, a new idea began to form. Seated on a rock, she grasped a stick and pushed a small pebble across the ground. This action drew her attention, causing her to abandon her thoughts and focus on the activity beneath her feet.

Perhaps it was a nervous twitch, but with a stick and pebble, she hesitated for a moment. However, after a few wrist flicks, she realized that she could fling the stone a greater distance than if she had thrown it herself. The pebble also had greater velocity added to it. It wouldn't take a genius to realize what the implication of her discovery might be, but in her case, an actual genius, she saw into the future. What she was picturing was the mechanical advantage of throwing a spear using a lever. If she could figure out how to make such a tool, maybe there would be less need for a healer whose practice was mending body and bone.

Chapter 7

Food Or Fire

Logic forced her to make a choice: food or fire. The current weather was bearable, yet they were unprepared for what may come, which could change as fast as it would take Mother Nature to change her mind. Food is something that can wait for the present; the children's care cannot.

She spent the time it took to gather sticks and pine straw, which she then piled outside their cave. "This is an ideal place for a fire," she thought. The presence of fire would keep predators at bay, and also shield the entrance to their sanctuary. Her head snapped toward the cave entrance. The silence was eerie;

had something happened to the children?

With one look, her dread eased; her newly adopted orphans were cooing and prodding each other with their small hands. She returned to the important task of starting a fire. At the moment the fire came alive, a noise at her backside alarmed her. She grabbed the biggest log of the pile and spun around only to see Drud approaching. He was dragging a giant sturgeon behind him. "So much for food," she thought. Looking at Drud, she felt the warmth of fire at her back; she turned and was amazed at how simple it was to create a fire to not only cook their meals but also how it formed a wall of protection.

With a deep breath, she steadied her nerves. It was time to share some of the skills learned in her clan. She picked up a large piece of flint and, with surprisingly little force, pressed it against a rounded granite rock. A satisfying crack echoed as a sharp slice of flint broke away, mirroring the precision and care her elders had instilled in her.

With the thick portion of the flint secured in her right hand, she sliced the fish down the length of its belly. It opened, spilling the large roe sac onto the rock floor. After removing the innards, she threw them onto the fire. She handed Drud her newly crafted flint knife and smiled.

Not like in today's world, where a young boy might take offense at the lesson a girl had given him, Drud almost smiled and accepted her gift, and within a minute, he had several pieces of flesh ready for the yet-to-be-made spit. Looking at Kara's pile of kindling, he chose two long sticks, weaved them through the flesh, and drove them into the ground. Placing the fish at an angle to the fire, they were moments away from their first hot meal.

While Chef Drud tended to the meal, Kara turned to the makeshift knife in her hand and visualized different ways she could create an assortment of weapons. After all, they were in the wild, and they had sacrificed their lives in the community's safety to save the children. She couldn't let them die due to her negligence. So after their first real meal, she needed to address the issue of weapons.

Sitting beside the fire, she started to chip away at her flint. Her first attempt involved knapping the style of point used by her clan. It was effective enough, but it shattered when it struck bone, so hunters needed to carry a lot of points. She thought that there must be a better design and was determined to find it.

Although her first points were Clovis type in shape and size, the design had its drawbacks, shattering just being one of them; another was its lack of aerodynamics due to the need to split a shaft and place the point in the split; it required a large amount of gut-string to affix it. That method was problematic, and failure sometimes led to the death of the wielder. They lacked the luxury of having other clan members to bolster their ranks in case of a hunter's death.

So, with that in mind, she began to knap a new and unique point.

Though Drud lacked communicative skills, he would express his thoughts by pointing a finger or thumping his thigh, sometimes a loud exaggerated grunt that she found annoying. Still, she and Drud began to talk in a way that only they could, which made the next few days possible. He smiled again when she shows him how to attach her new fluted point to a long shaft and how more effective it was than the old method. She returned his smile; laughter was a familiar sound in the Magnon's camp, unheard of within the confines of the Neanderthal's clan.

As soon as she had a spear that would fit her needs, and after throwing it, she realized that her strength was far less than that of Drud. Her thoughts returned to her stick and stone. What if she could propel her spear using a stick, adding mechanical advantage? When the spear refused to cooperate after several unsuccessful attempts, she visualized in her mind what might be needed to make it work.

She chopped a small twig off a dead tree and cut it to match the length of her forearm. She then added a notch near the end and fitted it to accept the spear's end. She made several more attempts at flinging it, and it just flipped in the air uncontrollably. Confused as to why it still did not work, she began to try different grips. When she placed her finger between the spear and the stick, creating an angle, the spear remained in its proper position, which allowed her to sling it forward. It wasn't a perfect pitch, but it did soar farther than just throwing it.

Drud watched as Kara manipulated her invention. He sat with the children, watching her intently. He had no idea what she was trying to do.

Kara had made several spears using the newly designed point. They were longer and thinner than the blunt points her clan employed and certainly more refined than those of Drud's people. With the glacier to the north and her clan's camp somewhere south of where they had found refuge, Kara set about proving to herself that there was a better way for the two self-imposed castaways to survive.

On a hill, a dead tree that had yet succumb to rot still stood with a bright blue sky as a background. Her movements were at first agonizingly slow as she struggled to understand the precise motions that would yield the best results. Remembering how her father would stand and at what distance from his target, she paced off fifteen steps from the tree and began to throw her weapon. She smiled; even for her, it was easy to hit the fat tree.

At the same distance, she knocked her spear, seating the end and placing her finger between the spear and stick. In a slow-motion movement, exaggerating her efforts to keep her projectile on a line, ensuring that it would not miss the tree, she released the missile. If there were a word or words that could describe her glee when watching her spear fly past the tree, it would be. "Yes!" Yeah, she missed the tree, but she was amazed at the distance it flew.

There was no laser ranging at her disposal, but she was positive that even though she was very deliberate in slinging the spear with her device, it appeared to travel through the air at a higher rate of speed than that of her throwing it.

After a dozen or more practice throws, she began to use greater effort and speed through full motion. Now it was time to target the tree from a greater distance. She was so confident that she increased the distance between her and the tree, by doubling it. Although she wasn't really gauging the wind, calculating the drop, or doing anything that resembled a sniper readying to pull the trigger, it looked as if so. A deep breath, a moment of doubt, and she let the spear fly using all her strength. She closed her eyes and listened to the spear tear through the air, and after what seemed to be forever, her eyes opened at the loud thud.

Her spear wedged in between the dead fibers, near the center mass. OMG! Or whatever was in play in their yet-to-be-created pre-religious lives, she might have screamed. With her eyes on the target, she emptied her quiver of spears. She then raced into the cave, and in a fit of joy, she dragged Drud by his arm out into her new and highly efficient reality.

She stood where she had tested her device and gave Drud one of her spears and motioned for him to throw it at the tree. He might not have understood what she wanted him to do because she was so excited. So she threw her spear at the tree without waiting. Undoubtedly, her lack of skill using such a lightweight weapon left him unimpressed. What good could it possibly be? Squirrels and rabbits were all he could think of, but that's better than nothing.

After his first toss, she moved him back five steps at a time until he had difficulty hitting the tree, missing on more and more attempts. Smiling, she took an additional ten paces to demonstrate her new invention. Unlike modern man, who would have mansplained how she had bested him, instead he smiled for the second time.

In their pre-Atlatl life, men of both clans suffered severe injuries during a hunt because of the short distance needed to satisfactorily bring down large game; her invention could give them a better chance of success. Ultimately, a single injury or death would reduce their chances of survival by half. Possibly now, they have a better chance of feeding themselves without all the associated dangers. Suddenly, the fear of predators hanging around their small encampment seemed less ominous.

Chapter 8

The Miricle Of Willow

Who knows who or when someone decided to weave long willow branches into a basket? It didn't matter. Kara had many skills, but her most exceptional trait was her ability to see others performing their clearly defined tasks and gaining knowledge from them. Although she has never made a basket before, she needed to give it a try. To hunt, they couldn't go alone or leave the children behind. So it came to be that Kara began to weave two small baskets that had two holes in them, which she could place the children in, and adding leather straps, they could carry them on their backs while they hunted.

She did not fret about the uneaten sturgeon left in the cave; if they were successful, it would not matter. There were several small herds of game animals grazing down the hill from their camp, indicating that food was abundant and ready for the taking.

In a normal hunt using old-world weapons, sneaking up on your prey was tantamount to full bellies. The problem was that over time, animals had developed an instinct that set off alarms and would cause them to bolt and, in a few steps, be out of range. That was not going to be a problem for our two backpackers.

They were 300 yards from their cave when they saw an Aurochs calf wandering away from the herd, dangerously close to the humanoids crouching in the deep grass. Kara felt no qualms at the thought of killing the calf; instead, she needed to express to Drud the need to strike at the same instant, hoping that at least one spear would reach the animal's flesh. Drud felt her hand on his shoulder; his eyes widened, and understanding strengthened his resolve. They stood in a low crouch and raised their weapons. With a nod of her head, two spears flew quietly through the air at an astonishing speed, with both striking the calf, one in the neck and the other penetrating its heart.

The animal fell to the ground in a graceful roll, nearly noiseless. Kara looked to the herd; only one bull Auroch lifted its head and just as quickly returned to munching on the thick grasses. Both hunters lowered themselves to the ground, removed their baskets, and set the children down. They cautiously moved toward the dead animal. Even though the calf was small, it was very heavy and difficult to drag over the thick grass. Even that movement did not alarm the herd; they continued to graze as the hunters dragged their meal back to the cave.

It was now Kara's turn to be impressed; Drud performed two seemingly effortless actions. Using a large flint, he disemboweled and skinned the animal, and when done, he held the animal high as if he were showing off his trophy. Spreading the hide beside him, he then laid the animals liver on it. His next step was to gather all the remains they wouldn't use, and remove them from the camp. After being away for a while, he returned and began slicing four strips of meat off of the thick thigh. He then threaded a long thin tree limb through each piece, arranging them into a pyramid of flesh over the hot coals.

He was not done yet; gathering large deciduous leaves, he wrapped all the glands, liver, and heart into a tight bundle and set it alongside the fire. Then he turned his attention to the guts. He stretched out the intestines to dry in the sun, alongside the stomach. He would cut the intestines into thin strips, and then braid together to create a rope. The stomach serves as an excellent water bag, reducing the need for frequent trips to the stream for water.

Once the meat trailing the spine had cooked, Drud carved out one strip and placed it on a flat rock. He portioned out the meat in equal shares, then cut off a small lump of it for the children.

Kara put one of the children on her lap; Drud did the same. They were seated by the fire; the smoke wafted up over the cliffside while coyotes wailed off in the distance; they had caught the scent of cooked meat. After little Drud began to choke on the meat, Drud removed it from his mouth using his finger, put it in his, and chewed the flesh until the bolus was easily swallowed by the hungry infant. Kara made a teenage face and followed suit. Once they had consumed all they could eat, they started the process of further cooking the meat into jerky.

Kara was impressed with how Drud managed their food stores. While she searched for more leaves, he washed and stretched the intestines. She returned with her repurposed backpack filled with leaves and dumped them beside Drud's pile of dried meat. Gathering more branches, she made a storage shelf at the back of the cave. Once they had caught up on their chores, which was a portent of their short-term future life together, they then sat and rested.

Unlike methods used by each of their clans, their approach to hunting did not frighten their prey off, which later would require a long day's march to find them again. Obviously, they could not continue to kill off all the calves; they would need to, at some point, bag a larger animal. With that thought in mind, Kara made larger spears along with a larger atlatl. She made the flints in the shape consistent with that of his clan. Hers were longer and thinner yet. In her mind, the sharper points would make up for what she lacked in strength.

Chapter 9

The Mending

Competition between the Magnons and the Neanderthals often resulted in perilous confrontations during difficult times. In the dry months, the herds that both clans relied on seemed to disappear; although it had been happening for eons, they drew no correlation between the climate and this strange disappearance. The concept of migration had yet to enter their thoughts. Although the skies were blue and the temperature was hot and nearly unbearable, Ando had to lead his hunters north into the hunting grounds of Erg, and that sometimes led to inevitable scuffles.

Before the introduction of meat in their diet, the Neanderthals subsisted on fruits, berries, and tubers. The advance of glaciers destroyed their main food source, leading them to incorporate meat into their diet. This set off a series of unfortunate events, ultimately leading the two clans to the only place on their shared land where they could find sufficient game.

Ando sat on a high hill looking over a small herd of Aurochs that may have been left behind when the main herd abandoned the area. He could see the shadowy form of the clansman he had met the night they both left their dying children in the boneyard.

They stared at one another for an extended period of time. They had no intentions of putting their people in harm's way. There were different reasons why they were hesitant; for Ando, the loss of another clansman would be devastating for those left in camp. For Erg, any loss of men would further worsen the clan's ability to support a practical existence. Suddenly, both men stood up and embarked on a lengthy walk around the herd, realizing the need for the clans to reconcile and unite for the benefit of them all.

Whenever the Neanderthals met after a long absence, a thump on their chest was their way of greeting. It was a message of a sort, showing the feeling of being glad to see you again, old friend. Neanderthals were rich in nonverbal communications, and the use of hand signals, grunts, and facial expressions was part of their language, they seldom used the spoken word. On the other hand, sorry for the pun, the Magnons would grasp each other's hand, not for the same reasons as those of the other clan. No, it was a defense mechanism and a lack of trust issue. Having another's hand in yours meant that you only had to watch one hand.

Both clans, which were sitting and standing on different hilltops, were confused as they watched their leaders move slowly around the herd to avoid scaring them. Neither group had any idea about what they were up to. The sense in both clans was that there would be a fight to the death. The Magnons were okay with the idea; if Ando won, then the others would naturally cede the hunting grounds to them, and all would be well. The opposite never crossed their minds.

The two leaders stopped advancing and stood, looking intently into the eyes of their counterpart. Ando bent at the waist, and laid his weapons on the ground. He stood and displayed his open hands, showing his willingness to trust him. Erg did the same. In the next half hour, the two leaders had made a pact through their innate ability to understand their inherent differences. No battle would occur, and the clans would cooperate in the hunt.

Both men returned to those waiting on the hilltops and explained how the hunt was going to go. The herd had congregated along a shallow where the dry grasses were thickest. The Neanderthals would enter the swale from the east while Ando would bring his men in from the west. Along the ridge on both sides, a contingent of hunters would wait and kill any Aurochs trying to climb the hill.

Without a signal, both clans moved forward.

Chapter 10

Are you seeing this

Kara and Drud were astonished at how their two clans had worked out a way to help each other. As the hunt progressed, the runaways watched from the entrance of their cave, while the two clans approached the herd from the low-lying ground. Meanwhile, a small group flanked the Aurochs from the opposite hillside, a strategy that made sense to Kara. Any panicked animal attempting to flee up the shallow hill would meet an armed band of hunters.

    Neanderthals are bashers and slashers, while the Magnons most often throw their light spears, thereby keeping a safe distance from possible harm. That difference could be the reason for the diminishing numbers in Drud's clan.

In Kara's mind, she found a potential flaw: the possibility that the panicked herd might actually rush the hill. The hunters did have an advantage at their elevation; the problem was that their numbers were insufficient. As if the world was listening to her thoughts, a large number of Aurochs turned away from the shouting marauders and raced to the top of the rise.

Four-legged animals have a tough time walking up an incline; it is easier for them to run at a gallop. The men's inability to control the panicked herd resulted in several fatally wounded men lying in the grass moments after the hunt began. Those who managed to avoid being trampled did kill three of the giant bovines. Once again, the duo watched as the remaining herd stampeded toward the Magnon's blockade, and like the hilltop hunters, they too took a terrible toll in clansmen losses.

While the herd, both on the hillside and along the valley floor, scampered away, the remaining hunters went to the aid of the injured. In order to help, Kara and Drud left their cave and descended the steep hill. "If only she could have told her father how they managed to bag one of the herd without alarming the others, maybe there wouldn't have been so many injuries," her thoughts raced through her mind.

While others collected the kills and dragged them to the center of where the herd was first grazing, a small contingent made up of both clans began to triage the injured, and there were many. Nearly all were from the Neanderthals; the cause for such was attributed to the way they hunted. Their learning of new methods has always been difficult for them to adapt. This fact suddenly became obvious to Erg; seeing the injuries compared to those suffered by the Magnons drove the problem home.

After tending to the injured and lighting a campfire, the first-ever inter-clan hunting-magic celebration took place in the hours that followed. The use of herbs was common during these events to thank earth mother for all that she provides. Lod would trade in herbs and medicines during their biannual gatherings when she could get her hands on a peculiar powder that had the ability to numb pain and, as an ancillary benefit, made the injured feel particularly good. It was during this celebration that no one noted that Kara and Drud were among the partygoers.

    Thar, a friend of Drud's, was shocked and fearful at seeing him dancing. He looked different because he was bigger than he had been when he had last seen him, and also because he and the clan had presumed him dead. A short second later, Miola caught sight of Kara dancing in front of the flames, and she let out a loud scream. She thought that she was seeing a ghost; she leapt and ran off onto the hillside, her hands were still wet with blood. Her screams brought the celebration to a sudden halt. A million natural events could have caused Mila to panic and run off into the wilds. There were only two unnatural things that would cause the same reaction, and the clans were looking at them now.

Ando was the first to respond to the apparitions standing at the perimeter of the celebration. With his spear at the ready, he hurried to his daughter's side, uncertain if she was still alive or one of the undead. He stopped and watched her; she was not frightened, nor was she acting like she was about to chase them from her otherworldly domain. He relaxed at her smile, dropped his spear, and embraced her. The Magnons drew a breath of relief, which was probably due to the intake of herbs. Not convinced that the Magnons were not playing games with them, the Neanderthals quickly gained their wits and drew their weapons. It got very quiet then.

Drud walked to the middle of the fray and stood. He set the basket with the young child in it on the ground by the fire. He extended his hand to Kara, and she responded by moving to his side. She removed her basket and set it beside the child's mate. She stood by Drud, and he placed his arm around her waist. Drud furrowed his brow, a symbol of threat within his clan that meant fight or back down. For her part, Kara approached her father and embraced him.

Ando was the first to break the mood and restore joy back into the day's events. He broke out into uproarious laughter, and that seemed to take the tension out of the air. In a normal world, an explanation would have ensued. An explanation such as "We thought you were dead!" or "The hyenas must have run off with the children," or a variety of other explanations for their sudden absence, would have been provided. Only after dividing the hunt's bounty would they need to work out those stories.

Chapter 11

Can You Count

Eleven was an enormous number for both clans to understand. Along with the Neanderthal hunters who partook in the hunt, there were fifteen Cro-Magnon hunters. There were thirty-one dead Aurochs piled around the fire. Neither leader had any idea how to divide the game equally. Kara took her father's hand, brought him to the edge of the fire, motioned for him to stand, and, with a scowl, warned him not to move. She then did the same to Erg, only he was on the opposite side of the fire. She stood back and was pleased with the space between them.

She then positioned the next hunter to the right of her father and gestured for him to remain in place. After realizing what she was doing, Drud grabbed one of his men and continued until there was a line on each side of the fire. There were eleven men to Erg's right and fifteen standing alongside Ando. Beginning with Erg, they dragged one Auroch to the feet of the stout leader and left it there. They next did the same, placing it in front of his counterpart. Once all the men on both sides had an animal positioned at their feet, there were still five more Aurochs left on the pile.

Without hesitation, the two arbiters placed the next four in front of Ando and Erg; it would be up to them to sort them out. One unassigned carcass remained for them to handle.

In a gesture of reciprocity, Ando removed one of his Aurochs to the feet of Erg. Moved by the gesture, the stout leader gifted him his cudgel. The gift found a warm reception, marking the start of a friendship that nearly ended before nightfall.

The Auroch carcass left on the ground and not distributed captured Ando's attention. Why was that left? Drud instinctively picked up the basket holding their child, Kara did the same, and they both then looked to their respective leader.

Neither needed to be a modern mind to understand what was happening. They were not returning to the clan, and the effect on Erg was chilling. Considering his dwindling clan numbers, the loss of even one member was cause for considerable concern. The conclusion of the hunt and the return of Drud filled him with joy, he truly missed him and how he had consistently provided help to the clan. Ando was, of course, delighted with his daughter's return, but it's clear to him that she has chosen to remain with the Neanderthal; unlike what Erg thought, he can live with that.

Erg couldn't. He crossed the distance that separated Drud from his clansmen, and he then tried to force him into returning to the clan camp. Two terrible things happened nearly simultaneously: Drud had grown in confidence since Erg had last seen him, he has been successfully independent during his time with Kara. He lashed out with a right cross and knocked Erg on his well-proportioned ass.

The second thing was that Kara, out of fear for Drud's life, had knocked a spear, and at the same time, Erg, reflexively, reached for a nearby cudgel and was in the middle of a deadly blow to Drud's head when Kara's weapon struck him in his chest. That was a significant setback, as both clans at once raised their arms in defense. Drud stepped between the frustrated clansmen and raised his arms, taking command of the situation.

In these ancient times, pragmatism prevailed. An all-out war between the elite members of each clan, positioned near each other, would plunge both clans into a state of crisis. Drud's temporary leadership brought relief to more than one member from each side. There was no need for more words or illustrations as they swiftly lowered their weapons.

Kara reacted to Erg's bullish behavior on instinct, not a conscious thought. Her next reaction was just as instinctual when she rushed to Erg's side and began to administer aid. The two clans circled the caregiver while she feverishly tried to stanch the bleeding. She quickly realized how effective her new point design was. In all her years of tending to dead game, she had never seen a point embedded as deep as hers. Of course, that presented her with the problem of saving his life.

Ando first withdrew and set aside the point. Then, despite the chaotic proceedings around him, he seized the point once more to thoroughly examine it. If there were a word to describe the utility of the point, he couldn't say; there were no words in their limited vocabulary to describe it.

Though Ando struggled to express his feelings for his daughter, his pride swelled. Succumbing to the reality of Kara's decision to leave their camp and start a life and clan with Drud was another source of pride. He not only is losing his daughter but also healer and a knapper of extraordinary skills. What else can she do? That is the reason he felt such a loss.

Erg is going to survive, and both clans will do their best to support life. Kara and Drud did one more thing that puzzled both clans. Aurochs are huge beasts, and the one in their possession now weighs in at nearly 1,200 lbs. Both clans circled the duo as they set about butchering the massive beast. That was a new experience for them. As a rule, both clans would drag their kills back to camp before butchering took place. Placing and securing the animal's skin over two long poles added to their confusion.

Even with mechanical advantage, 1,200 pounds of meat was more than Kara and Drud could manage to move to their cave. So, they devised a plan: they would leave the bones and a portion of meat for later retrieval. The two clans watched as they dug a shallow hole in the cool shade of an Elm tree and placed the wrapped portion of meat and bones in it. When time permitted, they could return to retrieve it.

Like the bearded butchers, using her long, thin stone knives, Kara began to fillet the meat. Her speed amazed the women of the clans as they wondered how she was separating the muscles into large slabs of lean meat so easily. While she was cutting, Drud made several bags of considerable size out of the stomach and intestines. The bones were placed in the biggest, which he tied to the bottom of the stake and leather sled. He stored the suet and tendons in the next larger bag, ensuring they were in their proper place.

When all was done, the extended flaps of untanned hide were tied over the butchered remains, and then a strap made of leather was tied to the leading grips. Kara touched her father's face, a rare show of affection. In this harsh environment, there was little time for appreciating one another. Still, bewildered by their preparations, as if a magic act had been performed, they all sighed when the two new clansmen hoisted the leather straps over their shoulders. With a pole in their hands, they began to trudge their way back up the hill to their cave, pulling the heavy load behind them.

Erg was still furious, but he was compelled by convention to let Drud go; this was always the norm and will continue to be so.

Ando understood the need for Erg to try to retain Drud; there was always a need for a smart hunter, and it appeared he's not only that, but he is also very effective. But the advances he has seen in just one hunt were overwhelming. Both clans needed to keep their prodigies in their home camps for the sake of their future.

Two unnaturally joined humanoids stood side by side and watched their future ascend the long and tortuous path leading to their cave. Every thought was to create a plan to bring them back into the fold.

Instead of shaking hands or acknowledging, each leader gathered their aurochs and clansmen and left the hunting fields. Ando looked one more time at his daughter as he bore witness to their ingenuity. Even after seeing how easily the two trailblazers managed their heavy load, although they did not butcher the animals, they did appear to have learned something. They started moving the weighty carcasses using modified methods. They piled some meat onto skins and that way they could drag many more slabs of flesh than they could carry.

Ando was not thrilled about losing his daughter; if he couldn't get her back, then he would be confronted with a situation that he had never faced before. Would it be the right thing to let them live out their lives away from the clan? Historically, the clan only allowed anyone to leave when its size increased and food availability became an issue. Once the clan reached saturation, a few members were portioned out, a leader was assigned, and then the newly formed clan was sent away.

These new clans would always head east, never the direction from where they originated. That was because the clans who had divided before would not welcome them. Leaving one clan was one thing; intruding into another's hunting grounds was another.

Chapter 12

End or Beginning

In the last few months, the two life-savers slept with the two children lying between them; tonight would be different. They sat on a rock and watched as their respective clansmen moved away from the blood-drenched valley. They marveled at the length of time it took them to disappear from view. Kara saw for the first time the vastness of their surroundings and their clear insignificance.

Both children were on the laps of their adoptive parents, quiet and peaceful. Kara was the first to react. She placed her child on a fur beside her; Drud did the same. She scooted next to him and slid her hand in his.

In a world of rugged landscape and untamed wilderness, two ancient beings had crossed paths in an unpredictable way. One had chosen to ignore the resolute life from which he was rooted, instead opted to join with a strange girl who was filled with unbound curiosity. He carried the rhythms of his clan's past experiences within his soul, while she possessed a newer, more powerful brain that glows brightly with the spark of innovation.

Love is not a feeling yet described in their world, but the power of their union affects the life in the steppes and beyond forever. Though they lack a shared spoken language and their differences are significant, they understand each other. Their dance of survival and adaptability impacts their lives, and their clansmen who are left behind. Theirs is the first, first love.

Made in the USA
Columbia, SC
13 May 2025